This book belongs to:

_____

A catalogue record for this book is available from the British Library

Published by Ladybird Books Ltd
80 Strand, London, WC2R 0RL
A Penguin Company

2 4 6 8 10 9 7 5 3 1
© LADYBIRD BOOKS LTD MMIX
LADYBIRD and the device of a Ladybird are trademarks of Ladybird Books Ltd

ISBN: 978-140930-244-5

Printed in Italy

Lewis Lion
Learns to Roar

written by Ronne Randall
illustrated by Jill McDonald

Out on the sunny plain, the Lion family lounged and lazed. Lions love to laze!

Lewis Lion loved lazing more than anyone.
He loved to s-t-r-e-t-c-h and feel the
warm sun on his back...

and his belly...

and even his bottom!

9

Mum and Dad were teaching Lewis
how to be a big lion. That meant
learning to stalk, prowl and pounce.
"Show me what you've learned,"
said Mum.

Stalk...   prowl...   pounce!

"Perfect!"
said Mum.

Dad was teaching Lewis to growl, rumble and roar.

Lewis opened his mouth wide, and gave a mighty *roarrr*!

"Just right!" said Dad. "You'll soon be ready!"

ROARRR!

But, although Lewis was good at lion lessons, his favourite time was when lessons were over.

Then he could snooze
and snore in the sunshine.

Lewis's brother and sister always
wanted to play.
"Get up!" said his sister. "Let's play
Leaping Lions!"
"Not now," said Lewis. "I haven't
finished napping yet!"

"Lewis!" called his brother. "Let's chase butterflies!"
"Not now," said Lewis, turning over. "I'm right in the middle of a wonderful dream!"

"What a lazy lion you are!" said Mum.
"When you are a big lion, you will
have to stay awake for much longer."

"Then I want to stay a little lion for ever," said Lewis. But he didn't really mean it.

Late one night, Lewis woke up suddenly.
His nose began to twitch. Something was
rustling nearby!

Lewis followed his nose into the bush.
He remembered what he'd learned
in lion lessons.
"I can be a big lion if I want to,"
he thought.

He *stalked*…and *prowled*…

…and he *pounced* with a growl and a

ROARRR!

"Boo!" said Lewis's little sister.
"Ready to play hide and seek?"
"In the morning," yawned Lewis.
"It's time for sleep."

The next morning, while the other young lions were having lion lessons and playing, Lewis had a lie-in.

"Shhh," said Mum and Dad, when the other cubs tried to wake him. "Lewis needs his rest. He's a big lion now. A special roaring, prowling night-time lion!"

Lewis smiled, sleepily. Not only had he become a big lion, he could still spend all day doing just what he liked best... sleeping in the sun!

29